Mrs Marvellous

HBAN
RE

First published in the UK in 2008 by
Two Rivers Press
35–39 London Street
Reading RG1 4PS
www.tworiverspress.com

Design: Sally Castle and Nadja Guggi

Printed and bound by CPI Antony Rowe, Eastbourne

ISBN 978-1-901677-57-7

Mrs Marvellous
Victoria Pugh

TWO RIVERS PRESS

With special thanks to Myra Schneider,
Michael Symmons Roberts, Susan Utting,
Paul Bavister and Lorna Patterson,
and to the many people who have helped me
and supported me.

Love God commended Scintilla poetry competition 2007,
published in Scintilla 11; *Blenheim Road* first prize Reading
Waterstone's poetry competition 2000, published in anthology;
Nature Boy, Face and *Touching* highly commended Blinking
Eye poetry collection competition 2006, published in Night
Balancing (anthology); *Talking cure* commended Scintilla poetry
competition 2005, published in Scintilla 9; *Sounds of the sea* and
Nude published in South magazine; *Llanddwyn Island*, published
in Plume; *The four-minute warning*, commended Reading
Waterstone's poetry competition 1997, published in anthology
(Two Rivers Press) 1997; *You are what you keep* prize-winner
(commended) Cardiff International poetry competition 1998,
published in New Welsh Review.

CONTENTS

For my family

MRS MARVELLOUS

Women weren't allowed in the magic circle until 1991,
when Mrs Marvellous squeezed inside.

She started with children's parties,
making packs of cards into concertinas,
producing bouquets of flowers that sprang apart,
secreting ping-pong balls in the sleeve of her jacket.

That wasn't enough.

She put her hand on a child's head,
conjured inner magic from behind his ear,
stretched the coils in his mind –
the pieces in between dropped out.
She showed him the folds in the night,
like the miles of villi inside him,
the way stairs unfolded as he stepped on them,
then folded up again.

That wasn't enough.

She took the circle from the atom bomb
folded it up, and folded it again,
made a fan to cool his face –
told him that bats' wings are broken circles;
the centre of a Catherine wheel
is the quietest place.

That wasn't enough.

She said she looked in his windows at night.
She was the past,
she'd grown out of a bush,
at one stage she'd been
a sort of centaur, half woman, half leaf –
pulling herself from a hedge
had been very painful.

That wasn't enough,
he wanted blood.

She lay in a tank
and pretended to drown –
stuck swords through her arms,
watched herself bleeding,
hung from a bridge and waited to drop.

She jumped from a crane –
was crushed on the pavement.

That was enough.
Thank you, Mrs Marvellous.

LOVE GOD

The man with the backpack of green things
walks down the path that crosses the earth.
He throws clover and grass on the track,
it grows up lush and sucks at his shoes
as he pushes them through the grass's spit.

He strokes the silver ripple on the wheat,
bends and enters the arch of white thorn
as the flowers endlessly tighten their grip;
throws stars from his pack, and they stick
in the branches and make heaven for us.

He sprinkles bitter fields from his bag
some Wild Garlic or Old Man's Beard,
burnt earth and stubble, many are fallow.
Then he's gone, somewhere, down the road.
He's emptied his backpack of green things.

BLENHEIM ROAD

On warm damp nights the snails ooze out onto Blenheim Road.
They do not sense anyone, or move out of the way,
they go where they are going,
and in the dark people step on them.
Walking on small cream crackers.

Sometimes, in the day, when the traffic stops and there are no people,
birds fly in formation along the road,
their wings beating in time –
the metre of their shared heart.
The simultaneous soft closing of books.

A path runs down through a spiral of leaves and opens up to the sun.
No one goes down it, and I won't use it yet –
I'll keep it up my sleeve,
A little piece of sleeping luck.
My leafy escape chute to a hidden land.

Two ladies layout their things and thoughts at the front of their house:
comments on global warming written on card,
a silver eel in a see-through bag,
a stag beetle in a jam jar.
A store of plenty – that's Blenheim Road!

SHELTER

Women walked past me
and boys kicked me after dark.
Seedy men offered me
a fiver, at a price.

I picked up my things
and walked through the town,
towards the wide grin
of the countryside.

I found the hollow tree
I played in when I was young –
crawled in with my bags,
and made myself at home.

And it's warm in here,
living in the oak's heart,
with the occasional oozing
of whatever sap that's left.

I climb up and sit in the branches,
and the oak and I
become a wooden Buddha,
with birds resting on our shoulders.

GOOSEBERRY

As we wander home along the river,
they'll always walk a little quicker.
I should go faster.

They will talk and I must listen,
this is the task that I've been given,
in this conversation.

Martha is pretty and must be heard,
Nita likes the sharpness of words,
so I will be quiet.

They talk about their latest men,
and how they want them back again,
now they've hurt them.

They can't imagine a man for me,
for someone who can barely speak,
cannot make a heart break.

The river purses his lips and ripples,
tells me things that make me giggle,
says my jokes are very subtle.

Martha and Nita – do as you please,
I've all the company I'll ever need.
The corn rears up and sings for me.

MOODY COW

The Children of the Sun have come.
When they open up their eyes
gold dust flies into the sky.
To understand their charms,
run your hand down their arms,
feel the butter on their skin,
and the life that burns within.
The Children of the Sun have come.

The Children of the Moon have come.
Put your cheek to their mouths
feel the frost on their breath.
When evening starts to cool
they wait beside the silent pool,
in the dark they start to swim
the rise and fall of moonlit limbs.
The Children of the Moon have come.

NATURE BOY

He decided to live in the city.
When his mother came to stay
she said he'd changed.
The flossy hair on his head
had turned to stubble.
His eyes had frosted over.

As they walked in the street,
he couldn't hear the grit
shifting in the buildings,
or see the smashed-up
fossils and corals, glowing
red and orange in the walls.

Not for him the under-wing
of the evening; or the diligent
zigzags of passers-by,
coming from their offices.
She left him fixed to a bench,
a statue in a sculpture trail.

She would think of him
as a young man, standing in
the speckled night sky,
his arms spreading outwards,
as the pulp of former lives
swelled-up inside him.

MOSS MAN

He stood in a clearing
surrounded by woods,
watching the moss
laid out across a rock –
sunning itself.
He rubbed it, and squeezed it,
then took out a knife,
levered it off like a pancake.

He laid it on his bare arm,
a skin-graft, stroked it like a cat,
and sat, like that, stroking it.

In the afternoon
he cut off another piece of moss,
and another, and sewed them all together.

He danced as he put them on.
"I'm in your skin, I'm in your skin,"
he chanted as the sun went down.
As soon as he stopped moving,
the bracken shot up through his shoes.

ON BARNES COMMON

No one knows who left the sofa in the woods.
The fleecy fabric is torn and the rest is faded.
The creamy foam is watermarked with grime.
Brown bones stick out from beneath the foam.
She is sitting there, patting the seat on the sofa.
It would be easy to say yes, sit down next to her.
Smile as the bindweed curls around my fingers.
Watch strangers stepping out from the darkness,
lit-up briefly by the streetlights beyond the trees.
I'd be near them, though they couldn't see me.
I could hear the cars pass by, the sirens calling.
The cars would fast-forward, into one long line.
We'd sit here, she and I, and have a cup of tea,
press the remote control, and stare into infinity.

THE DANCING GIRL

The dancing girl skips down the street,
whirls her arms in a Catherine wheel.
She dances her kerb and gutter jig,
and stares at the sky open-eyed.
Smiles and waves at the trees and houses,
aware of nothing but her pleasure.

Children shout at the dancing girl,
"You're daft you are, you're mad."
Soon she'll only dance her jig
when she forgets what people think.
She will not smile or wheel her arms,
ignores her contact with the stars.

The girl has now become a woman,
doesn't want her special gifts.
What's she done with the dancing girl,
who could not understand the world,
laughed and danced and stared at the sky?
She keeps her locked away inside.

WAR GAMES

The aircraft carrier moves across the squares –
with water swirling out behind,
stops midstream and waits.

Satellites watch over the Ark Royal,
can show precisely where it is.
You don't know.

Your submarine moves up to F4.
The voices of the world speak through its radio.
I can't hear them.

My battleship's a blip, it's dipped
below your radar.

*

We drive for miles, not knowing where we are –
someone on the furthest star
could find the answer.

*

You're overlooking Cardigan Bay.
You phone to say you're lost,
somewhere on the coastal path.
With every landmark you mention,
I follow you on the map,
know better where you are than you do.

*

I try to pinpoint your position
on the John Speede map on my wall,
wonder what you make of the two-dimensional hills,
the sea-monster with two spouts,
what it's like, walking inside
the imagination of the mapmaker.

Watch out! Tudor battleships, bigger than Aberystwyth,
are crowding round the coast.

THE MOLE-GOD

I rushed in, dropped everything, read your note:
It said, "I've gone to find out about the mole God."
Then the phone went. When I'd finished talking,
I thought of you, setting off in your safari hat,
crawling through all those tunnels – then stopping,
wondering if you were looking in the right place,
if the ground above was mole-equivalent to sky.
Instead of clouds you'd gaze at trees or traffic lights.

I read the note again, this time turned the page:
It said, "I've gone to find out about the mole God
put on my back! We'll need to talk about it later."
I think you already know where the mole-god lives.
You're staring in its face. I wish you could've found
something brown and velvety, crowned with glory.

FACE

We are sitting, trying to touch, but not touching.

I want to say to you,
that your head seems perched on your neck.
Your chin looks strange –
your face looks like it could slip right off.

That you could wear your face like a badge,
on your jacket. You could work it with strings
and make it say you were happy.

All the time the real you would sit behind,
saying nothing, while your mouthpiece talked.

And the difference between the real you,
and your mouthpiece, would be the distance –
exactly equal to the distance between you and me.

When the world speaks to you or I speak to you,
you take no notice. I will take off your badge
and turn it around, so it is facing you.
And this time, you will hear it.

TALKING CURE

Sometimes I feel very small.
I'm lying on the carpet of the world.
My back is pressed into the earth.
Giant poppies are growing overhead.

I know you understand.

You always wait so patiently,
ready for me, in the early morning,
when I'm polishing the green corridor.
The nurse sleeps behind the counter.
Then, you and I, we can talk.

Your hand's like a bird's skeleton.
Mine's etched with brown lines,
dried-up rivers in the sand,
pink half-moons in my fingernails.
You always squeeze my hand,
to let me know you can hear me.

The nurse says you'll die soon.
What does she know?
She thinks life is a bird,
trapped inside your rib-cage,
fighting all the time to be let out.
I don't think so.
It's like water being poured
slowly back into the earth.

I touch the folds of your face,
ridges of sand on a wind-blown beach.
I think powder will come off in my hands.
It doesn't, but I see the places
where my fingers pressed,
though I touched you very gently.

I stroke your hair,
the endless surf on the coast of Africa.
I put your hand in my beard.
You curl your fingers in there.
I wonder what you think of my skin.

And I tell you,
I don't know why I left my home,
and came to this country.

Yesterday the nurse came.
She told me to go away,
that you were more awake.
Your relatives are coming,
though I've never seen them.
You won't want to know me any more.

But I've crept in here, just for a moment
and I see that you are crying.
You lift your eyelids.
This is the first time I have ever seen your eyes.
They are two small blue worlds.

You say, as you smile at me,
and stroke the hairs on my wrist,
"Sometimes, I felt very small,
I was lying on the carpet of the world,
my back was pressed into the earth.
I'd look up and see the sun's face."

ALL THAT GLISTERS

The escalators pour down from the first floor,
and splash in the glass bowl of the entrance hall.

Shoppers step on, and glide down the silver stairs,
a stream of queens, or ancient popes on rollers.

Jerseys in packets are colour cards in secret corners,
navy for town, green and purple on the grouse moor.

Buckles, black patent handbags, buttons and cutlery,
flicker out their message – " Buy me, I'm shiny."

Gold make-up on lit-up counters – polish and pearl,
bronzing and blusher – "You too can be beautiful."

Through the doors to the caff in the staff quarters.
Stale coke drips from seats and sticks to the walls.

Men ogle the new girl and like the size of her tits.
Women say, "I hate my boss, she's such a bitch."

Ladies put away cardigans and pairs of smelly shoes;
and then they slam their locker doors as they go.

SHOP FRONT

The shoppers look through the window at the clothes.
They don't see the green tiles shining,
or the arch of Art Deco flowers
moulded across the top of the shop front.

Gaze at the green squares for a while and touch them.
Squeeze the sunlit feathery moss,
glazed by a veil of water,
that lives somewhere inside these tiles.

Stand and watch the garland of flowers, and listen.
Blue tulips with grey play-doh stems,
bend, and open up their heads,
and say, "Who made me, who made me?"

THE SCRIBBLED MAN

There was a man drawn on her fence,
just shoulders and the back of his head.
She passed him on her way to work,
in time she became quite fond of him.

She even went to the back of the fence,
wanted to check that he had no face.
She nagged him to tell her what he saw,
until he said, "The inside of the fence."

She painted him on a wooden box
then locked some secret objects in it.
She asked what he could see in there,
he said, "It's a different kind of inside."

He began to walk in front of her
or maybe he had always been there.
As much as she would inch around him,
he'd inch around the same amount.

She asked him if he knew some place
where half-things find their other part,
so she could see his face, see inside,
know for once the business of a leaf.

She took his hand and made the leap
into the silver at the back of the mirror.
When she got there, and saw his face,
it wasn't at all as she'd imagined.

RICH PATTERN

The silver path is stitched inside the bracken.
It weaves and wanders across the marsh,
through the limelit coral strands of lichen.

Clouds sink and surround the mountains.
In winter the owls hunt across the earth.
The silver path is stitched inside the bracken.

The misted lights on the station platform
fade as he walks on the marsh's path,
through the limelit coral strands of lichen.

He wants the secret of the spider's pattern.
He grabs her web and he steals her heart.
The silver path is stitched inside the bracken.

Her dewy knots and threads are broken.
The bulrushes jabber as he goes past,
through the limelit coral strands of lichen,

The marsh's fabric frays and weakens.
The springy earth softens as he departs.
The silver path is stitched inside the bracken,
through the limelit coral strands of lichen.

LIVING IN COMFORT

Creamy rock was broken into stones,
that scraped arms and took off skin.
They were piled together to make the walls
that marked the course of the lanes.

To build the house, stones were cut in blocks,
laid on each other, ribs set between them,
holes filled with mortar, rubbed down,
covered with plaster and paint.

*

When Annie first came with Martin
she covered herself with body lotion,
in case there were places in her
that he'd find wanting.

The creases in the folds of her arms
and behind her knees began to deepen.

*

She took her children on a trip to London.
They ran to an underground platform,
as a train was waiting.

Her son jumped in.
Doors clumped shut.
She shouted through the glass.

She found him at Earl's Court
and he was fine. She wasn't. She'd seen
a crack in the universe that anyone can fall in.

*

The day before they left the house
she looked through the photo albums.
She smiled at the faces, searched for her life
in the sugar-paper between the pictures.

Another couple moved in.
They stripped away layers of paint,
plastered, puttied, sand-papered,
glued-up new paper and painted again.

The walls mark the course of the lanes,
scrape arms and take off skin.
Snails live in their crevices,
gliding over the stones that grate like pumice.

SOME COMFORT

Squeezing the chrysalis, the thing inside
still crawls out before it dies, longs to fly –
though not yet born, knows its mind.

The gnarled bark of the apple tree begins
to open up as the rain seeps in, pushing
flesh apart. It will heal and grow again.

EVERGREEN

There's a shortcut to the top of his garden.
He steps on a low wall, covered in ivy –
trodden down by years of his diligence.

His footprint is set in woody stems,
squashed flat, while around his mark
the plant continues to grow.

On holiday, he wanted to go home.
He stood by his car, in the rain,
waiting for his wife to drive him.

The slanting rain battered his face,
ran down his back, used him as a gutter.
He didn't move or look for shelter.

The shortcut in his garden is still there,
but the ivy is scrabbling along the wall,
just in case there's another footfall.

SOUNDS OF THE SEA

Inside, right down in there,
you found out something about me.
It's covered up, you can't see it.

You heard it,
as you lay next to me.

Not my heart, not my pulse,
but the silver strands that creep through me,
gathering force.

Sand eels whimper under the rocks.
Peeler crabs shiver in their shells.
The bass are sick of butting through the surf,
and head for deeper water.
The wrasse fold down their turquoise fins,
and hide beneath their ledge.

The sand beats round at the bottom of the ocean,
spinning up to reach the surface, until
the sound inside me is too hard to bear.

Only you could hear it.

TOUCHING

Your hand rests on the table.
It's brown and marked, large and solid.
If I touched it,
I'd feel the roughness of it.

I watched you once rub lavender stalks,
between your palms,
and when you touched my face
they smelt of summer.

Without a single word,
you put your hand on my knee.
Feel my skin –
it's tougher than it used to be.

But if you made yourself small,
you could crawl round
to the soft place beneath,
and stay there very comfortably.

And as you lay there,
you'd hear the sea push through me,
or touch my veins,
and feel the purple seaweed swish by.

If you leave your hand on top,
the soft flesh of your palm
and the warm place beneath my knee,
will never meet.

LOCK AND KEY

He found a box under her bed,
an old wooden box with a lock.
At first he ignored it.

Sometimes he heard it creaking –
the wind still ran through
the branches it was cut from.

He pulled at the lid and scratched it.
Soon he noticed the wood
had grown around the gash.

The edges of the lid and the sides
of the box grew outwards,
making a pair of wooden lips.

He ran his fingers across the lips,
knotted, dry and comforting,
like the mouth of an older woman.

He spoke to the box every day,
kissed it and begged for its secret,
until the lips drew back.

When he saw the sappy wood
he ripped it and the box opened
with the hiss of a tree being cut.

There was nothing in the box.
When she saw it was broken
he had no one to talk to, no one to kiss.

STORING PERISHABLE ITEMS

To stop the trickle of stars to the ground,
take cling film and wrap it all around them.

Tip the stars in a bowl, place in the larder
on the cold black shelf, more film to cover.

They'll wait till everyone's gone to sleep
doze in their bowl like peppermint creams,

then thump their feet, then fly in the air,
like ice-white moths at an unseen barrier.

They know in their hearts that it is pointless,
they fizzle in the darkness nevertheless.

As star-drips fill the bottom of the bowl
stars float and jostle until they dissolve.

Perhaps they're best kept somewhere else,
shoved in the sugar jar on the kitchen shelf.

ANGER MANAGEMENT

His mouth is wide open with anger.
Some slimy thing lives in him,
and it's coming out, right now.

It shoots out of his mouth,
a serpent, that dives into her mouth
and slides right down.

He's OK, he spat it out –
it's one less animal to care about.
He's closed his mouth now.

He can open it any time
he'll be just fine. But from now on,
she'll keep her mouth shut.

She thinks the serpent's gone,
crushed by something in her stomach,
run off to some desert.

It's only later, oh, so much later,
she looks inside, and finds it,
coiled around her heart.

IT CUTS BOTH WAYS

The little bristles on his chin
were so sharp
they pierced her heart.
Now they rub her
up the wrong way.

NICHE

He could have chiselled
her initials on a tree,
left them there for all to see,
instead he tattooed them on his knee.
Even when he knelt to propose
he knew exactly where she should be.

BLOCKBUSTER

There are films clips running in my head.
There's one I keep rewinding.
I play it again and again.
Though I try to manipulate it,
it always comes out the same.

It's our last time together.
I'm hoping you'll say you cared for me.
I go over the things you said,
or didn't say, and hope next time
I play it, you will say it.

I've a grainy clip, with no sound.
You're walking in your garden.
You're burying something.
It's cold out there, but you're happy,
busy, putting everything away.

I'm making a film about someone,
his bare arm's just like yours.
I zoom right in to the side of your wrist,
those dark hairs packed together –
a soft little goatee beard.

I've a still of you in your kitchen.
I'm near, but we're not close.
You had a choice of company,
you preferred your cold streak to me.
It did what you said, and didn't talk back.

OUTERWEAR

My clothes kept me safe,
with them on I was brave.

I always wrapped up warm,
against the shade of a man.

You said I'd won your heart.
I took off my hat and scarf.

Your face began to swim
through my bits of open skin.

You needed to feel my touch,
my gloves came off at once,

you held my hand so tight
I could not wave goodbye.

You said it wouldn't hurt me
as you peeled away my shirt.

I'd made myself too soft.
You didn't like me when my clothes came off.

BISCUIT MAN

I'll put you in a shortcake tin,
green, with scotsmen round the side,
marching as they play the pipes.
It's at the bottom of my larder.
I wanted to choose something nice
not dull or made of tupperware,
a friendly box to lock you up in –
my man in a biscuit tin.

And as I try to shut the lid,
your eyes shine below the rim,
changing from hazel to bluey-green;
and your little voice begins to cry,
"Oh, please don't shut me in."
And I must never peer inside
or you might use that look again,
make me think you really cared.

I'm told I must forget the past,
but you keep tapping on the tin,
trying to remind me how I felt,
shouting, "Let me out, let me out,"
and I must never say, or think,
that I'd like you to let me in.
One day you'll crumble into dust,
and then there'll be no more of us.

DAWNING

She was sleeping, and he touched her hair,
and for a moment, he was standing near her.
She woke to find the sea-light on the walls,
then watched it trickle out beneath the door.

VIEWPOINT

I was standing on the top of Scout Scar.
It was winter and the light was fading,
though the sun still warmed the small of my back.
All around the snow picked out
the pink tops of the mountains –
and I thought about your open hand
and your fingertips
that first time.

It's summer and I'm here again.
The tops of the fells are cut-outs in the sky –
and I have thought about your curled hand,
ever since then. I am unbearably sad,
but I think I can understand,
why you closed it.

NUDE

Blood spots like red-currants,
dot the skin across your stomach.
Crows have flown from your eyes
and left their footprints behind.

Red thread-worms cross your cheeks,
your nose is their meeting place.
When the light shines on your hair
your skull shows up beneath.

Your heart line and your lifeline
are overwritten a hundred times.
Those grey hairs cup your face –
as, perhaps, his hands did once.

The holes made for your earrings
have wriggled down your lobes,
weighted with the faded pearls
he gave you, as he held you close.

Silver earthworms stripe your hips
and mark your breasts like starfish.
In the cold, the soles of your feet
have cracked apart, and they bleed.

As you sit there, under siege,
you smile. You are beautiful.

FRIEND

The night after you died I saw you,
standing by the bedroom door.
I held you in my arms.

We were beautiful, our bodies perfect.
You were just as you had been,
when we were young.

And we were truly naked with each other,
naked as we never could be,
when you were in your skin.

LLANDDWYN ISLAND

We walked along the curving beach to Llanddwyn Island,
picked out ahead of us by the pinky rays.

It's a headland, not an island. Saints and souls
lived here and loved this place.

We reached the rocks at the end and perched on a ledge,
our feet could touch the top of the sea.

A school of mackerel zipped around the island, we saw
their skins flash pink and green –

their bodies pushing up above the water – I could
skate across their backs to Nefyn.

The moon and stars came out and laughed, as we stumbled
along the crescent in the darkness.

THE FOUR-MINUTE WARNING

We were lying in bed
on a sunny, Saturday morning
when the siren sounded.

We held each other for a
while and considered our last
few moments on Earth.

We thought of hiding under
the table, or painting the
windows with black paint

in the end my husband
brushed his teeth and I
changed my daughter's nappy.

When the siren stopped
we waited, and we waited –
nothing happened.

We walked into town, and
followed crowds of people
down to the River Kent.

The Kent was flooding – nearly
over its banks. The water
rushed through the town –

thundering in the sunlight;
surrounded by shadowy
mountains and blue sky.

Small trees, logs and debris
rolled past us. At any
moment I expected to see

a Canadian logger leap
from log to log, wave,
and shout, "Nice day."

At home I said to my neighbour,
"Did you see the flood?"
Later I heard her say

to Mrs Ottway, "These offcomers –
one small flood and they
think it's the end of the world."

YOU ARE WHAT YOU KEEP

"They're weird, these people,
look in the box, it's full of teeth."

And he emptied the box of teeth
all over the bed.

He pulled out a drawer
and tipped the contents on the floor.

He found:

A pendant made of plastic
with a crab trapped inside it.

A small seal
made of real seal skin.

A badge that played a song
and lit up when he turned it on.

A postcard of dolphins at Knossos.
A photo of dolphins at the zoo.

Something that was very gooey
in a coin bag from the bank.

Caked make-up by Mary Quant.
A candle, a pencil, a thimble, a buckle.

An extremely small copy of Macbeth.
A card saying Happy Bithday, Mum.

He ripped open a bag and found
a plaster cast of someone's teeth.

"They've got nothing, just nothing."
He threw the teeth at the wall.

They left by the back door –
he threw my rubber gloves on the floor.

HOUSE CLEARANCE

Time stepped from somewhere under the stairs.
They didn't seem to know he'd been waiting,
curled in brown paper at the back of pictures,
in the imperfections under layers of paint.
He scrawled in the dust between the banisters,
tiptoed to the window to watch the world drift.
Years passed and they noticed his stifled laughter
his cobwebbed hand reach for the light switch.

Now he's in the larder, with out-of-date cans
and mouldy pots of jam. "Everything must go,"
he shouts – they don't hear him, they've shrunk
from the world that's flying past their window.
At last, it's their turn to slip between the boards,
weigh down the dust that lives beneath the floor.

RIVER WARRIORS

Indian women in white saris
ride on white horses
in a clear, sparkling Ganges.

Water soaps the horses' necks,
the saris stream out behind.
Brown legs grip white backs.

They ride in the day and night,
and in the twilight, their clothes
turn a very pale violet.

They are riding from Benares,
an army of Indian amazons,
showered down from heaven.

A boy runs along the bank,
shouting, "Where are you going?"
The women say nothing.

They force their way upstream,
back to the Himalayas,
to melt into their ice cave.

VICTORIANA

She points her foot and steps into the world.
The sky is muddy brown – it will snow soon.
She has ringlets and a muff around her neck,
a maroon top-coat and black lace-up boots.
She smiles as she slides on the icy pond.
Snow falls as white coal, that turns to icing.
Sheep walk to the sunset, coats many-coloured,
oiled by the reflection of the setting sun.

She lands on the back of the deer as it runs.
The sky is purple as it touches the mountains.
She likes her riding habit and ankle boots,
her tartan hat with a feather sticking out.
The heather, the turning trees, the lake below
are glossed with gold and made from velvet.
The stag stops, he knows the end is coming.
She wept when the world left her behind.

ROMANCE AND REALITY

I was standing by the Cold Meats counter,
staring at a choice of plastic hams.

I heard an announcement on the tannoy.
Someone was calling for 'Mr Wickham'.

I thought: Oh, I need you Mr Wickham.
though I'm not fifteen, more forty-five –

please whip me away from Dairy Produce,
stride through the crowds around Frozen Food,

your long coat flapping behind you,
your high hat way above the shoppers,

your boots snapping on the floor tiles,
slapping your hand on your muscular thigh.

Grab my trolley and cast it aside.
Declare your undying love for me –

or at least for my wallet of credit cards.
Kiss me; and whisk me away to London.

HAMLET STRIKES BACK

She ran all the way to the station,
missed the train to Paddington.
And then the tube was late again.
She couldn't find the Barbican.

Five minutes late for Hamlet.
She was told off by an attendant:
"Don't go in, you must go down,
wait, in the Late Comers' Lounge!"

She missed the first appearance,
of Old Hamlet on the battlements.
She watched the play on video-link,
until she could make her entrance.

That's the trouble with Hamlet.
He's always thinking of doing it,
waiting for the right moment,
some time soon, but just not yet.

As she watched the television,
in the theatre's stark waiting-room,
she knew that she took too long
to do things she should have done.

She had spent her life sitting,
in time's Late Comers' Lounge.
She got to her feet in an instant.
Now let the performance begin.

NOT HOT AIR

I've laid out my words in front of you.
Set them out in white porcelain.

They'll clink as you pick them up
and store them, one on top of the other,
in your cupboard.

I've buried my white words in the sand.
They'll float up one day, wash along the shore
like bleached shells for you.

I've planted my words in your garden.
Each year they'll pop up on your lawn,
tenacious as daisies.